WHEN STARS COLLIDE

A short story by

Zoran Stanic & Dan Rendell

Cataloguing-in-Publication entry is available from the National Library of Australia http:/catalogue.nla.gov.au/.

This edition first published in June 2024
Hackham, South Australia.

ISBN   paperback   978-0-6459991-2-9
       ebook   978-0-6459991-3-6

Story by Zoran Stanic
Written by Dan Rendell

Typesetting and cover by Ben Morton
Cover art by Alem Coksa
https://www.deviantart.com/alemcoksa

Published in Australia by Immortalise via Ingram Spark
www.immortalise.com.au

WHEN STARS COLLIDE

A short story by

Zoran Stanic & Dan Rendell

Inspired by actual events

Chapter 1

THE PROBLEM WITH NOAH

When two stars merge or collide, they might create a new and brighter star, called a blue straggler. Noah Riley always wondered about such things, like whether it was possible for two souls, destined to spend eternity together, could in fact merge, like two stars, and exist as one. Noah was a dreamer; he was what you might call an old soul.

Born and raised in the American town of Huntbury, his father, Victor Riley, was an officer in the Army; and his mother, Janette, was the CEO of a large weapons manufacturer. They were better off financially than most, but life for Noah wasn't as happy as you might expect.

Noah's parents barely had time for their son, and even when they did, they were always out getting drunk at parties. His parents showered him with presents and money, but all he really wanted was their time and love. He wanted his father to take him camping or fishing, as opposed to buying him the latest gaming console.

You see, Noah didn't care much for expensive things. Well, that's not entirely true, there was one thing. The one thing they couldn't separate him from was his 1965 Mustang convertible; a graduation gift from his parents. Noah had always been obsessed with classic cars. But his parents didn't buy him the car because they knew he would love it. They were hoping it would prompt him to get out of the house and socialize more. But Noah was an old soul; old souls are deep thinkers and often struggle to socialize with most people, who are often worldly and materialistic. Noah's grandmother had taught him traditional values, and that love was more important than money.

When he was seven years old, Noah's grandfather died and his grandmother moved in with them. Not in the main house, but in a small flat out back. With both of his parents working, Noah's grandmother was his strongest influence. She wasn't well-educated, and had spent most of her life as a stay-at-home mum. She was caring and loving, fiercely devoted to family, and was known for her good common sense.

She taught Noah that money didn't necessarily make one happy, and that life wasn't supposed to be about how many 'things' you could accumulate over a lifetime. Noah's grandmother gave him the time and love he so desperately needed.

However, not long after his sixteenth birthday, Noah's grandmother passed away. The morning after the funeral, Noah didn't come out of his bedroom for the longest time. His weeping was endless. His mother knocked on the door a couple of times throughout the day, asking if he was alright. Through a muffled voice Noah would say, "I'm fine. I just want to be alone for a while."

With his grandmother gone and his parents always working, Noah had no choice but to look after himself. Yet, despite their busy jobs, his parents continued to enjoy their party lifestyles, leaving Noah at home alone. But since his grandmother's passing, all he could think about was being self-sufficient, just as she and his grandfather had been in their youth.

Noah would sit in his car for hours and wish he could visit the past, and live out his life in a simpler world. He wanted to live in a world that wasn't obsessed with technology and materialism, so Noah decided that he was going to attend college and complete a course in sustainability. With his heart pounding, Noah went to the lounge room, where his parents where quietly watching the television.

They both looked up at him as he approached. "Mum, Dad, I'm going to go to college and learn about sustainability."

Victor and Janette turned to each other in silence. Noah swallowed hard as Victor slowly sat up, pressed the mute button and stood up. "Son, your mother and I have worked too hard to see you throw your life away. You're going to go to college alright, but you're going to be a doctor or a lawyer."

Noah gritted his teeth. "I don't want to be a doctor or a lawyer. I don't want to spend my life chasing money. I want to live the way that Grandma and Grandpa did."

"I knew his grandmother had something to do with this," said Janette, standing up. "Noah, we know how much you loved Grandma and Grandpa, but their lives weren't easy."

"That's right," said Victor, "living on a farm isn't easy— it's hard work. Do you really want to spend your life digging in the dirt and cleaning up animal crap?"

Tears welled up in Noah's eyes. "You think I don't know that, Dad? Not once have you ever taken me camping, or fishing, or hiking, or anything meaningful. Grandpa did all those things with me."

"You think we haven't taken care of you?!" Victor barked. "You've always had a roof over your head, three meals a day, and the best education that money could buy. You've never had to go without! If your mother and I hadn't worked so hard, do you really think you'd be able to go to college? You wouldn't have the education, and you certainly wouldn't be able to afford it, would you?"

Victor took a deep breath as tears began to stream down Noah's face. Janette looked at her son with concern. "Noah, your father and I just want what's best for you."

"It's your mother's fault," said Victor, looking at Janette. "She's the one who filled his head with all that farming nonsense."

"It's not nonsense!" Noah cried.

"Calm down, Sweetie," said Janette.

"No!" he cried again. "I'm going to college to learn about sustainability, and that's that! And if you won't let me, then I'm never going to college at all."

His parents watched as Noah stormed back to his bedroom and slammed the door. "What are we going to do?" asked Janette, turning to her husband.

Victor slowly nodded his head. "If that's what he wants—fine. Don't worry, once he realizes how difficult that farming stuff is, he'll come around."

Noah spent the summer at home. He waxed and polished his car in the driveway every day, while listening to the radio. He hadn't caught up with a single friend since graduating, not that he had many friends. One night, as they sat down at the dinner table, Noah was about to reach for the salt when his mother said, "I have a surprise for you."

"Huh?" Noah looked up, his hand still halfway to the salt.

"I've arranged for some of your old school friends to take you out for a night on the town! They'll be here within the hour."

Noah's eyes widened. "Is this some kind of joke?!"

"Hey! Don't talk to your mother like that!" said Victor. "She just wants what's best for you—we both do."

"Then why didn't you ask me?"

"Because you would've said *no,*" his mother replied.

"That's right!" said Victor. "I mean, all you do every day is wax and polish that damn car! Don't you think it's clean enough?"

"That car is a 1965 Mustang convertible, and you bought it for me—for my graduation. Or did you forget? It must be hard for you to keep track of all the gifts you buy me so you won't have to spend time with me."

His father shook his head in frustration. "When I was your age, I was out every night with my friends. We took girls to dances, went to theaters and concerts, they were the best days of my life. You've spent the whole damn summer at home waxing the car. We didn't buy it so you could wax it; we bought it so you could get out of the house and have fun. You've only got a week before college, so make the most of it."

"You bought it because you didn't want to feel guilty about being at work all the time."

"Your mother and I work hard to provide a good life for this family."

"Family?!" said Noah. "This hasn't felt like a family since Grandma died."

"Look, we all miss Grandma—"

"You never understood her. She actually knew what was important."

"Your Grandma and her 'common sense and decency,' belonged to a different time."

"She taught me to take care of myself, and it's just as well, because you were never going to do it!"

"Noah!—" Victor bellowed.

"Noah, your friends will be here soon," his mother interrupted.

"Who did you call, anyway?" he asked.

"Oh, just Troy and the rest of your old gang."

"Troy? I haven't spoken to Troy in four months. I guess I shouldn't be surprised that you don't know who my friends are."

"Please, Sweetie," said Janette, "we want you to be happy; we want you to have lots of friends. Just go out tonight. Who knows, you might meet a nice girl!"

"Fine, I'll go. Just leave me alone."

Noah took his plate to the kitchen and quickly ate some of it on the way to the sink. He was nervous about going out, especially with his old high-school buddies. Noah's friendship with them had been based mostly on his fear of not fitting in. He left his plate on the sink and went upstairs to quickly shower and change.

Chapter 2

THE CLUB

His four friends, Troy, Mike, Brad, and Dale, picked him up on the hour, just as his mother had arranged. They took him to a local dance club. His friends rushed to get inside, leaving Noah to take his time. As he entered the club, he was hit with the powerful aroma of perfumes and alcohol.

As he became enveloped by the thick darkness of the club, the thumping music began a throbbing headache in his temples, which was only aggravated by the flashing lights. There were twice as many women in the club as there were men, and two of his friends were already chatting some of them up. Noah spotted the other two at a table in the back and made his way there. "There you are," said Troy. "What took you so long?"

"It's dark in here, that's all."

"I'll get us some drinks," said Mike, before leaving the table.

Troy stared at Noah. "I didn't think you'd come out with us."

"To be honest, I didn't want to. I just did it to shut my parents up."

"You should've heard your mom on the phone!" Troy laughed. "I had her on loudspeaker. Mike almost busted a gut from trying not to laugh."

"Why? What did she say?"

"It's best if I don't repeat it. Your mom thinks there's something wrong with you. I think she's worried that you'll never leave home and she'll be stuck with you forever."

"What else did she say?"

"She said you're going to college, but that you don't want to be a doctor, you want to save the whales or something."

"I don't give a damn about whales—I just wanna learn about sustainability."

"Whatever floats your boat," Troy scoffed.

They sat until Mike returned with their drinks. "Vodka for us, and a juice for Noah!" he smiled. "Your mom told us not to let you drink too much alcohol, since you probably have a low tolerance!" he snickered.

Noah didn't reply. He just lowered his head and took a sip of his juice. Mike and Troy quickly downed their vodka shots and headed for the dance floor. They didn't bother asking Noah if he wanted to join them. "What have they done to this?" Noah grimaced, holding up the glass of juice. "It tastes like cat piss!"

Glancing at his friends, Noah saw they were having a good time. Mike was already kissing the girl he was dancing with. *How can he do that?* Noah thought, *He probably doesn't even know her name.*

He listened to the music but couldn't hear the lyrics. Every song sounded the same, like drums beating against his head. The flashing lights made him nauseous, and his headache was becoming unbearable. As he looked around, Noah couldn't help but notice how drunk and out of control everyone was. They were acting like a bunch of sex-starved animals.

Before the end of the first hour he couldn't take any more. Standing up, Noah began to make his way towards the exit. "Hey, where're you going?!" he heard Troy shout.

He glanced back but continued to leave. Then, out of nowhere, a girl stepped in front of him, blocking his path. "Hey, handsome!" she said, pushing herself up against him and wrapping her arms around his neck.

"Excuse me, but I was just leaving," he replied.

"I've been watching you," she smiled. "You haven't danced with anyone yet."

"I can't dance."

"Okay," she said, "then at least give me a kiss before you leave."

As she opened her mouth to kiss him, Noah was struck by the smell of vomit and marijuana. "Get off!" he cried, breaking free of her.

Noah left the club. He made his way to the car park as quickly as he could, trying to distance himself from the sounds of the club. Approaching the car, he heard a voice behind him, "Noah! What's wrong with you?! That chick was hot!"

He turned around and realized his friends had followed him outside. "Her breath smelled like vomit," he replied.

"That'd do it for me!" Mike laughed.

"Not me!" said Brad. "I'd still give her a go!"

"Hey," said Dale, "let's go to that burger joint near the petrol station! I got a text from Kelly Sharp. She's there with her friends right now."

"Girlfriends?" said Brad.

"Of course, Dopey!"

"Then what're we waitin' for?" said Troy.

Noah couldn't help but notice how intoxicated they were, except for Brad, who was the designated driver. With the music blaring they headed off in Troy's car. They sang along to the rock music as they went. Mike kept sticking his head out the window, yelling and barking at several women as they drove by.

Finally, Noah had had enough. "Stop the car!"

Brad slowed down and pulled over. "What're you doing?" said Troy.

"Noah told me to stop."

Noah climbed over Mike to get out. "What's wrong?" asked Mike, "Are you sick?"

"I'm going home," he replied.

"Why?!" said Troy.

Noah sighed. "Because I'm not interested in getting drunk, hooking-up with random strangers, or doing stupid things, like barking at women. That's not who I am."

"What, you think you're better than us?" Troy scoffed.

"That's not what I said," Noah replied.

"You know what, I think your mommy's right! You are a misanthrope! She's probably gonna be stuck with you forever!"

"Yeah!" Mike laughed. "I bet that chick's breath didn't even stink—he was just afraid to kiss her! Weren't you, Virgin?"

Noah stared back at them, and said, "I hope you all have a nice night."

Turning away, he headed along the sidewalk, towards home. As Troy's car drove by, Mike stuck his head out the window. "Go back home to Mommy—loser!"

Ignoring them, Noah continued to walk home. It was a beautiful night. The air was fresh, and every now and then he would hear the hoot of an owl. It was a three mile walk home, but for Noah, it was the best part of the night.

Arriving home, the first thing he saw was his mother sitting on the couch, drunk. She was talking on the phone while watching TV.

"Just a minute—" said Janette, taking the phone away from her ear. "Hey, Sweetie. You're home early! Did you have a good time?"

Noah stared at her blankly. "Yes, Mom, it was the greatest night off my life," he replied. "Where's Dad?"

"Oh, some work thing. He'll be back in a few days."

Noah headed up to bed, he felt like crying. *There has to be more to life than just sex and partying...* he thought. *Those guys were never my friends. I'll never have any real friends, and I'll never have a girlfriend either, because there's no one else like me...*

Feeling helpless, Noah got out of his clothes, put on his pajamas, and hopped into bed. Turning off his lamp, he laid his head down on the pillow. "I just wish life wasn't so fast," he whispered. "I wish I could've lived in Grandma's time. I just want to be self-sufficient."

Chapter 3

LUCY

Hoping his college course would open the flood gates to self-sufficiency, Noah spent the rest of the week reading up on agriculture and sustainability. Before he knew it, it was Monday morning.

Noah didn't recognize anyone from high school. His first week of college started off quite badly. He was hoping to learn something that would aid him on his quest for self-sufficiency. But his teacher, Mr. White, seemed more concerned about telling his students how awful humans were for the planet, as opposed to teaching them anything useful.

By Friday morning, he was feeling depressed and disgusted. *I came here so I could learn about being self-sufficient. But all this guy wants to do is brainwash us with his climate-alarmist bullshit! I get that things need to change, but he's not offering us any kind of solution,* he thought.

As soon as it was lunchtime, Noah was first out the door. He still hadn't made any friends. All the students he had spoken to, seemed to have lapped-up everything Mr. White said, as if they had no minds of their own. He now felt that he wasn't at college at all, but some kind of left-wing indoctrination camp. Noah hated how everything had become so politicized. He couldn't imagine being friends with anyone in his class, but someone had noticed him, even though he hadn't noticed her.

Sitting on the grass, Noah was about to bite into a peanut butter and jelly sandwich when a pair of beautiful, sandal-covered feet appeared in front of him. Her toes were painted with blue nail polish, and she was wearing a lovely blue dress. Looking up at her, Noah was captured by her beautiful brown eyes. "Hello," he muttered.

She smiled at him. It wasn't a small, everyday kind of smile, but a big toothy one, as if she had been looking forward to meeting him all week. Her skin had a golden tan and her long brown hair was tied back in a knot, with a yellow flower sticking out of it. "Hi, Noah. I'm Lucy, Lucy Collins," she said, reaching down to shake his hand.

"How'd you know my name?"

"What, you didn't notice me?," Lucy gave him a wry smile. "We've been in the same class all week. May I join you?"

Noah was hesitant but gave her a nod. Sitting down beside him, Lucy looked at him with another smile. "Are you okay?"

"Yeah," he said, defensively. "Why do you ask?"

"I've been watching you. You always sit by yourself, and you seem really sad. Sometimes it helps to talk to a stranger."

"I doubt there's anything you could do. I came here to learn about sustainability and how to be self-sufficient, but

Mr. White seems more concerned about expressing his political views than he does about offering up a real solution."

"I know what you mean," said Lucy.

"I feel like quitting," Noah tore out a tuft of grass and then let it blow away in the wind. "It's just so…" he sighed and looked at his shoes.

"But," Lucy waited until he looked up at her eyes. "the world's so amazing and beautiful. If you try, you can get the best out of it, no matter what anyone says, especially when you're young."

Noah glanced down at the grass. "I don't see anything beautiful about it."

There was a long pause, but when he looked her in the eyes again, Lucy said, "The world may have its problems, and sometimes we feel helpless to do anything about it, but you are young! Embrace everything life has to offer while you still can. Find what makes you happy and hold on to it forever! If you have goals, then do what you can to achieve them, so that one day you won't be sorry you missed out."

"What am I going to miss out on?" asked Noah, unable to look away.

"One day, you will be old, maybe in a wheelchair, and life will be passing you by, and you'll only be able to watch it. You won't be able to enjoy it, like now, when you're young. You'll just be waiting for someone to wheel you around."

Noah's eyes widened. "You know what, this is the first time I can remember when someone has told me something that's absolutely true!"

Lucy smiled, staring deeply into his eyes. "There's going to be a party at my house tomorrow afternoon. Would you like to come?"

Noah's heart sank when he remembered his night out at the club. "Will people be drinking alcohol?"

"No," she replied. "My parents will be home. They don't allow alcohol in the house. It's more like a gathering than an actual party, but it'll still be fun."

"Okay," he said. "I'd love to, thanks."

"You're welcome," she smiled.

Lucy wrote down her address, the time of the party, and her phone number on a piece of paper and handed it to Noah, then left him to finish his lunch. Noah's head was spinning when he returned to class. He was sitting in his usual spot by the door, but couldn't stop glancing over his shoulder, where Lucy was sitting at the back of the room. She would always smile, as if her eyes were on him constantly.

When he arrived home, Noah went straight to his bedroom. He sat on his bed and smiled. He couldn't stop thinking about Lucy. "She's changed my whole outlook on life. Maybe the world's not as bad as I thought?"

Noah realized he was smiling; it was the first time he could remember. He used to believe that all girls were like his mother, and just drank and partied, without a care in the world. He also used to believe they weren't deep-thinkers, and had no empathy, like those of his grandmother's generation did. For the first time in his life, Noah believed he had found another old soul.

Meanwhile, back at Lucy's house, Lucy burst through the front door with a spring in her step and a smile on her face. Her parents were fascinated by her behavior as she danced about the kitchen, humming and singing a lovely tune. "What's got into you, my girl?" said her mother, staring with curiosity.

Lucy went into the lounge room, where her parents were seated. "Oh, mother! I met the most wonderful boy today! He's sooo cute! I've been watching him all week! Today, I finally had the courage to speak to him!"

"I hope he's a nice boy," said her father.

"Oh, yes! He's nothing like the other guys at college, looking for booze and sex. He's shy and quiet, and he wants to be self-sufficient—I just know he's a deep-thinker, like me! You'll see!"

"What do you mean?" asked her mother.

"I invited him to my party!" she smiled. "I can't wait for you to meet him!"

Chapter 4

TWO STARS

Noah parked his 65' Mustang at the front of the house. He checked the paper in his hand; the address was accurate, yet the house seemed quiet. Noah had been expecting loud music. Lucy's house looked plain enough. It was a typical suburban dwelling, single-storied, with a two-door garage and a white picket fence. Noah rang the doorbell. "They *are* playing music…" he whispered to himself, hearing the faint noise inside.

The door opened. "Noah!" said Lucy, with a big smile. "Come in!"

"Hello," he replied. Stepping inside, Noah handed her a box of cookies. "You said there wouldn't be any alcohol, but my grandmother always said it was polite to bring something when you're invited to a party."

"Oh, thank you—they look wonderful," said Lucy, closing the door. "Come, let me introduce you to everyone."

He followed her into a big lounge room. There were eight guests, plus an older couple, which he assumed were Lucy's parents. He didn't recognize the others. They were having a discussion about sixties music when Lucy and Noah approached. "Hey, guys, this is my friend, Noah. We share one of the same classes at college."

One by one, Noah was introduced to the guests, but he soon forgot their names. In truth, the only person he wanted to talk to was Lucy. Then she introduced him to her parents, who were sitting on a lounge together. They seemed like a nice couple, and he could sense that they were looking forward to meeting him. "Hey, Dad," said Lucy, "now that everyone's here, can we start the barbecue?"

"Sure," he said, standing up. "Why don't you bring your friends outside and we'll get the fire-pit going as well. There're plenty of chairs. We can always turn up the music, too."

"Great!" she smiled.

They gathered in the backyard. The music was turned up and some of the guests began to dance, while others simply sat and talked. Noah spoke with some of them, and was able to have deep, meaningful conversations about the origin of life, philosophy, and the future of humanity. "So," said Lucy, "are you glad you came?"

"This is exactly the kind of party I've always wanted to go to," he replied.

"See!" she smiled. "The world isn't always what you think —it's what you make of it."

"I'm really glad I met you."

"I'm glad you said that, because I feel the exact same way," she said, with a spark in her eye.

Noah watched as Lucy brought a red apple to her lips and took a big bite. She smiled, and was soon offering him a bite. Taking the fruit, Noah took a big bite out of the other side, piercing its soft, red flesh with his teeth. "Where did you get this?" he asked. "It's delicious!"

"From our tree," Lucy replied, turning her head toward the back of the yard.

Following her gaze Noah noticed the apple tree in the back corner. "My grandparents had apple trees on their farm," he stated.

"I wish I lived on a farm," said Lucy. "I'd love to have some fruit trees, a vegetable patch, chickens, and maybe some cows. What do you think?"

"Sounds like heaven to me," he replied.

"Do your grandparents make their own fruit preserves?"

"Yes, well, they did. They've both been gone for some time," Noah replied.

"Oh, I'm sorry," said Lucy.

"That's okay," Noah sighed. "I wish you could have met my grandmother. She would've liked you. You kind of remind me of her."

"Really?" Lucy smiled. "I bet you learned a lot from your grandparents. I'd love to have a big cellar full of preserves one day."

"My grandmother showed me how to can fruits and vegetables. Perhaps one day we should can some of the apples from your tree?"

"I'd love that," said Lucy.

Noah took a deep breath. "Um, would you like to go on a picnic with me? We could drive up to the mountains, where it's quiet?"

Lucy stepped closer to him. "Well, I'm busy with family stuff tomorrow, but we could skip college and go on Monday?"

"Okay," he whispered, "but don't tell anyone. My parents would kill me if I skipped college, especially when I've only been there for a week."

"My parents would kill me, too!" she said, struggling not to laugh. "It'll be our secret."

Noah spent the rest of the evening dancing with Lucy by the fire-pit. Their connection was becoming stronger with each passing moment, as if some supernatural force was at work. It was difficult to leave the party, but when Lucy kissed Noah on the cheek and said goodbye, he thought he was going to melt.

Monday morning couldn't come soon enough. Noah got up extra early to prepare everything. He packed cold lamb sandwiches, some canned sodas, red apples, and a nice blanket to sit on. He placed the picnic basket in the back of his car and left the house at 7am. He picked up Lucy at the front of her house. Her parents waved them off, convinced that he was driving her to college.

They left town and headed for the mountains, where the air was fresh and the grass was greener. They were happy in the car as they talked and laughed. Their emotional chemistry was flowing like a river, making them feel closer and closer. They stopped by a quiet meadow and picnicked beneath the shade of an oak. They hardly ate anything, and couldn't stop talking, looking, and touching each other. It was like they had been pre-ordained to fall in love and be together forever.

For several hours they remained, grateful to be in each other's company. When Noah finally built up enough courage to kiss Lucy on the mouth, they could barely restrain themselves. They made out for what seemed like an eternity, as their souls became intertwined. Finally separating, they decided to take a drive up the tallest mountain so they could see the whole forest and surrounding meadows.

Driving up, with the sun shining and the top down, they continued to talk and laugh. They barely knew each other, yet they were already in love. "Where're the apples?" asked Lucy, glancing at the back seat.

"On the seat behind you," Noah replied. "Can you get one for me, too?"

Lucy reached around, opened the basket, and managed to grab a couple of apples. She took a bite of hers. Then, teasingly, she put Noah's apple close to his mouth and pulled it away as he tried to take a bite. "What're you doing?!" he laughed.

Lucy took another bite of her apple. Then, with half of it sticking out of her mouth, she kissed him, allowing him to eat from her. Sitting back, she handed him his apple as Noah proceeded to take a big bite.

Lucy stared at him as they continued to drive up the mountain. "I think I've fallen for you, Noah Riley. I hope one day, when we are both old, that we can be sitting on a nice porch together, watching life pass us by."

Glancing at her, Noah could see the deep love and longing in her eyes. "I wish that too. I wish that more than anything…"

Chapter 5

THE APPLES OF DEATH

The warm summer breeze was caressing their faces as they drove up the mountain. The surrounding forest was full of pine trees, and the curves in the road were becoming more dangerous. Noah handed his half-eaten apple to Lucy. She took a big bite as he slowed down, preparing for the next bend.

The approaching bend was elevated, and as Noah slowed, an enormous truck appeared out of nowhere carrying a load of massive logs, and traveling way too fast. Noah's mind raced as the world seemed to slow to a crawl. He glanced across at Lucy and immediately saw the fear in her eyes— they both knew what was about to happen. Noah tried to swerve and avoid the collision, but to the left there was nothing but cliff-side and the right he could see nothing but empty sky; there was nowhere to go.

The eighteen-wheeler hit the side of Noah's Mustang, pushing it off the side of the mountain, with a force so powerful that Noah and Lucy were thrown from the car. Their bodies rolled down the mountainside as the Mustang crashed and tumbled through trees.

After regaining control of his enormous vehicle, the driver of the truck managed to stop. Rattled, he slowly got out. He surveyed the scene, but couldn't see his young victims. Noah's car was also gone, having landed at the base of the mountain among the trees. The driver looked around for witnesses, but, of course, there were none. After kicking a few pieces of broken glass off the side of the road, the driver quickly left the scene without reporting it, never to be seen again.

Many months passed. By all accounts, the young couple, along with Noah's car, had vanished into thin air. Both victims' parents were devastated, but the police had no leads. Eventually, they came to the conclusion that the young couple had run away together. Noah's parents thought it was possible, but Lucy's parents could never believe such a thing. They knew their daughter would never run away without letting them know she was okay.

Twenty years later, there still hadn't been any news of the missing couple. Their bodies were now covered by two and a half feet of mud and dirt, caused by a mudslide. Despite the loss, both parents had accepted that Noah and Lucy's disappearances would forever remain a mystery.

One day, an old man came back from Italy. He'd been away for twenty years and had returned to visit his neglected block of land in the mountains. He was hoping to clear his land of trees and build a cottage for himself. He spent three days clearing the land.

The grass on his neglected block was very high, and there were many trees and bushes. Unexpectedly, at the base of the mountain, he came upon two apple trees, bearing ripe fruit! "Son!" he cried. "Look at these!"

His son quickly approached and stared in amazement. "Did you plant these, Papa?"

"Of course not!"

"What should we do with them?"

The old man stepped forward. "They are so big and healthy-looking. I think we'll leave them be for now."

Three months later he had finished his cabin and was glad to be spending his first night on his once neglected property. The next morning, at 3:33AM, he was awoken from a strange dream. He dreamed of a young couple having a picnic beneath the apple trees. They were drinking, laughing, kissing, and feeding each other. He thought it was an odd dream, but soon went back to sleep.

Every night, however, he was awoken at 3:33AM by the same dream, repeating over and over again. Sick of the dreams, he decided to dig up the apple trees, hoping it would put an end to it. It was very early, and the air was thick with mist. The sun was just peeking above the tree line as the old man began to dig. After digging for about ten minutes, he was shocked when he came upon a large bone.

He ran back inside and called the police, who sent out a forensic squad. It wasn't long until two skeletons were uncovered; the roots of the trees had grown over the bodies, covering them like a shroud. After being informed about the state of the bodies he crossed himself.

And after conducting a search of the surrounding woods, the police discovered Noah's mangled car buried at the base of the mountain, less than twenty yards from the apple trees. Personal items were also recovered, including his wallet. The police contacted the parents of both children; after twenty long years they had finally been found.

Their parents visited the old man's property and thanked him for the grim discovery. Grief was in the air, but at least now they knew. Though he was hesitant, the old man felt it was necessary to tell them about the dream. Lucy's parents were certain it was a sign from their daughter, but Noah's parents were more skeptical.

Finally, a forensic specialist approached. The expression on his face was one of shock and bewilderment. He wiped his forehead with a white cloth, took a deep breath, and said, "First, I'd just like to offer my condolences to you all. We've finished our investigation of the remains, and as far as we can tell, it seems that before your children died they used their final precious minutes to comfort each other."

"What do you mean?" asked Lucy's mother, with tears streaming down her face.

"Well, Ma'am, as you already know, both bodies were found together, and Noah's hand is still interlocked with your daughter's right—I've never seen anything like it."

All the parents began to weep. Lucy's parents approached Noah's parents, and Lucy's mother said, "Our Lucy was so happy the day she met your son."

Noah's parents continued to weep in silence. The most they could give was a small nod. Still, they were glad that Noah didn't die alone, and had experienced great joy in meeting Lucy.

Both parents asked the old man if they could replant the apple trees as grave markers, feeling that their children should be buried together.

He agreed. When the police released what was left of their bodies for burial, Noah's parents spared no expense in making sure the trees were transported to the town cemetery. It was the most unique, costly, and mournful funeral at that time.

Chapter 6

THE BLUE STRAGGLER

Word traveled fast and Noah and Lucy became legend. People were convinced that the ghosts of the young couple were still together, enjoying their afterlife. With the world watching on, they were laid to rest in the town cemetery, in the same fashion they had been found, but with something extra. Between the trees, they set a white, wooden cross; the crossbeam touching the trunks of the two apple trees, with their names inscribed on each end.

The elaborate grave was visible from the highway, and over the next few months, many people claimed to have seen a young couple sitting beneath the trees, having a picnic together, just like in the old man's dream. Not being conformed to the world and against all odds, Noah and Lucy found each other. And exactly one year, to the day, after the couple had been laid to rest, a rare celestial event occurred in the sky above. And as the people looked up and watched the wonder of two stars colliding, they were reminded that some souls are indeed destined to be together… forever.

THE END